THE WICKED FAIRY-WIFE

The Wicked Fairy-Wife

A FRENCH CANADIAN FOLKTALE

RETOLD BY
Mary Alice Downie

ILLUSTRATED BY
Kim Price

Kids Can Press • Toronto

Kids Can Press acknowledges the generous contribution of the Canada Council and the Ontario Arts Council in the publication of this book.

Canadian Cataloguing in Publication Data

Downie, Mary Alice, 1934-
   The Wicked Fairy-Wife
   A French Canadian Folktale

ISBN 0-919964-53-2

I. Price, Kim. II. Title.

PS8557.085J32   j398.2'09714   C83-098555-7
PZ8.1.D69Je

PRINTED IN CANADA by The Alger Press

Book Design by Michael Solomon

Kids Can Press, Toronto

For Charles, Una and Charlotte

ONCE upon a time there was a poor old farmer who had a wife, four children and not much else. One night his hut caught fire and burned to the ground. The old man wept as he sifted through the ashes.

"What shall we do, my good wife? We have nothing left but each other and our children."

They left their ruined home and trudged along the king's highway until they came to a small cottage. The old farmer knocked on the door, but there was no answer.

"There is no one here," he said to his wife. "Let us spend the night."

The next morning the family searched every corner of the house, but it was empty. There was not even a stray cat to be found.

"Surely the owner would not mind if we lived here until he returned," said the old man. And so they stayed. For three years they farmed the land and were happy together.

Then one day a stranger came along. "Good day, monsieur."

"Good day," replied the farmer.

"Tell me," asked the stranger, "what are you doing living in my house and farming my land?"

"Kind sir, please don't make trouble for us. I am only a poor farmer. When our hut burned down, my family and I found refuge here."

"Then you do not know whose house this is," said the stranger.

The old man shook his head.

"I am Prince Nicolas, the king's son."

"Noble sir, you are rich," said the old man, falling to his knees. "Have pity on a poor man."

Now among the four children was a lively young girl named Josette. The king's son noticed her gentle smile and beautiful brown eyes and fell in love with her at once.

"Give me your daughter," he said, "and I will give you my house and my land."

The old man was heartbroken, but he knew what he must do. "You will be rich and happy with the king's son, my daughter. Go and God bless you."

The prince gently helped Josette into his carriage and off they drove. When, at last, they reached the city, Josette's eyes opened wide at the sight. The royal castle blazed golden in the sunlight.

"Look after her as if she were a princess," the king's son ordered the servants. He hired the finest teachers and singing masters to instruct her. Josette learned her lessons well. She was treated kindly and was happy, and with each passing year she grew taller and more beautiful.

One day the prince called her forth. "Josette, it is true that I took you from your parents, but I have had you well-educated and cared for. Now I want to marry you."

"Monsieur, you are mocking me," Josette cried. "I cannot wed the king's son, for I am only the daughter of a poor farmer."

"But I love you and I want you to be my wife. We can be married at once, if you wish."

So they were married. Messengers travelled throughout the kingdom proclaiming the wedding. All the high and mighty in the land put on their finest robes and hurried to the castle to join the celebration.

Josette's parents lived a great distance away and could not come. But on the wedding day they toasted the bride and groom with blueberry wine.

After the wedding, the young couple settled down and lived happily together. One morning Prince Nicolas said to Josette, "My dear, it has been many years since you have seen your parents. Today we shall pay them a visit to tell them our joyful news."

The prince ordered that his four black horses be harnessed to the carriage and they set off right away. As they passed through a small valley, Josette saw a lace tablecloth lying by the side of the road.

"Husband," she said, "do let me pick it up."

"But, my dear wife, we have many tablecloths at home."

"That one is very handsome. I want to take it as a present to my parents."

The prince leaped from the carriage to fetch the cloth. But when he picked it up, what should he find underneath but an ugly old crone who grabbed him by the throat.

"Marry me or I'll strangle you," she croaked.

"My good woman, I cannot, for I am already married. There is my wife sitting in the carriage."

"That one!" squawked the old woman. "She's only fit to be a servant. Marry me or I'll strangle you!" and she tightened her grip.

Josette, afraid for her husband's life, begged him to agree.

The old crone, who was really a wicked fairy, climbed into the carriage and pushed Josette aside. They returned to the castle at once.

The fairy made Josette wait on her hand and foot while she lay about eating raw lemons. Every day Josette scrubbed and cleaned the castle, but that was not enough. At the end of a week, the fairy woke up one morning in a dreadful temper. She cursed and swore and broke every plate in the castle.

"That girl is not learning a thing," she screamed. "I want to be free of her. I want her hanged."

"But she is my wife," stammered the king's son.

"None of your buts," the fairy raged. "I am your wife now. Send for the hangmen, or I will tear out your eyes."

The next morning the four hangmen led Josette into the forest. "How can we kill this poor young girl?" they asked one another. "Let us tear out her eyes instead."

"Dear God!" Josette wept. But she knew that it was better than dying.

So the hangmen plucked out her beautiful brown eyes and left her sitting, alone and despairing, on a tree stump.

When Josette had wept all her tears, she sat listening to the rustlings and cries of the forest. "If I stay here," she thought, "I will surely die. Perhaps I can find shelter somewhere in the woods."

She stumbled off with her hands before her face. Soon she heard the sound of an axe chopping wood. "Who is there?" she called.

"It is Jean-Paul, the woodchopper."

"Dear sir, please help me," Josette begged. "Guide me to your house, or I will die of hunger."

"Poor soul," he cried. "I will do what I can." So he piled his logs in the cart and sat Josette in the middle. Then he signalled to his weary old horse to take them home.

"Who is this?" Madeleine, the woodchopper's wife, demanded when they came to the hut.

"A wretched young girl who called out to me in the woods."

Madeleine, too, took pity on Josette in her distress. "Poor child," she said gently. "Come inside. We will look after you."

She helped her out of the cart and led her by the hand into the hut. Then she washed Josette's wounds and gave her food.

Josette did not tell her story lest the wicked fairy discover that she was still alive. She pretended that she was a widow who had been set upon by robbers while on her way back to her family in a distant part of the kingdom.

"But I must not travel now," she told the couple. "May I remain with you until my baby is born?" For that was the joyful news that the prince had wanted to tell Josette's parents.

And so Josette stayed, helping as best she could and singing songs at night to entertain the woodchopper and his wife.

Several months later Josette gave birth to a healthy little son whom she named Jean-Paul after the woodchopper. She and the child remained with the kind-hearted couple for many years.

Josette taught her son all she knew. The boy grew into a fine young man who could trim a tree, sing a song, and add a sum better than anyone for miles around. But he grew restless with their quiet life.

One day he asked his mother, "Why do we live hidden away in the woods?"

"I cannot tell you that, my son," Josette replied.

"Why don't I have a father like everyone else?" he asked.

"I cannot tell you that, my son," Josette sighed.

"Why were the eyes plucked from your head?"

At this Josette could remain silent no longer, and she told Jean-Paul the story of his father and the wicked fairy who had ordered her hanged.

"I am going to find my father and take revenge upon the fairy for her wicked deeds," he cried.

"It is too dangerous, my son," Josette said.

Despite his mother's warnings, Jean-Paul set off at dawn. He walked and walked until he came upon an old man who had a tuft of white hair tied back by an eelskin. The man was sitting on a stump by his cabin door, watching his axe chop wood.

"Good day, sir," Jean-Paul called.

"Good day, my boy. You look weary. Come and rest."

"But I have a long journey before me," Jean-Paul said. "I am looking for my father."

"That's interesting," the old man said. "What is his name?"

"I don't know. All I was told is that he married a wicked fairy who ordered that my mother be hanged. The hangmen took pity on her and tore out her eyes instead."

The old man lowered his voice. "Come inside," he said. "You look like an honest lad, so I will help you." He gave Jean-Paul supper and a bed for the night.

In the morning, before he sent him on his way, the old man served Jean-Paul a hearty breakfast. "To find your father, walk along the highway until you come to a fork in the road." The old man handed Jean-Paul two small cakes. "Eat these, think of me and your way will become clear.

"When you come to the city, go to the golden castle and ask to be taken on as a servant. Your father is now the king there. He will not know you, so pester him until he agrees. Good luck, my lad."

Jean-Paul set off. When he reached the fork in the road, he ate his two small cakes and thought of the old man. No sooner had he done so than the way became clear. He came to the city and saw a splendid castle glittering in the sunlight.

"Good!" he said to himself. "This is it," and he knocked on the door.

"Who is there?" called a mournful voice from within.

"Please sire, I am a poor orphan and I have come to ask the king to take me in. I can trim a tree, sing a song, and add a sum better than anyone for miles around."

"I have one servant already and that is enough. Go away."

"Let the boy in if he is willing to work," ordered the wicked fairy, who was listening at the door.

The king shrugged and opened the door. He looked tired and woebegone, for since the loss of his beloved Josette, he no longer cared what happened.

Jean-Paul was pleased. Things were beginning well.

The wicked fairy made Jean-Paul wait on her hand and foot, and for a time she was satisfied. Then one morning, she woke in a rage. She cursed and swore and broke every goblet in the castle.

"That boy is not learning a thing," she screamed at the king. "If he does not bring me the horse with the grey beard by daybreak, I want him hanged!"

The king felt sad, for he had grown used to Jean-Paul's cheerful ways, but there was nothing he could do.

Jean-Paul left the castle at once. He walked and walked until he came upon the old man who had helped him before. The man was still sitting on a stump watching his axe chop wood.

"Good day, sir," Jean-Paul called.

"Good day, my boy. You look weary. Come and rest."

"I have a long search before me," Jean-Paul said. "I must find the horse with the grey beard and bring him to the castle before daybreak, or the wicked fairy will have me hanged."

"Never fear," said the old man, lowering his voice, "I will help you." So he gave Jean-Paul supper and a bed for the night.

In the early morning, before he sent him on his way, the old man served Jean-Paul a hearty breakfast. "Take the first turning in the road," he said. "Walk on until you come to a field with an iron fence where you will see twenty-five ferocious lions. They are guarding the stable of the horse with the grey beard."

The old man handed Jean-Paul two small cakes. "Before you put one foot over the iron fence, eat these and think of me. Then be careful not to make a sound.

"When you enter the stable, you will see three bridles. Do not touch the silver or brass bridles. Take the bridle made of good steel, put it on the horse with the grey beard and all will be well."

Jean-Paul thanked the old man and set off. He followed all the instructions carefully. Before setting foot over the iron fence, he ate the two small cakes and thought of the old man. Instantly all the lions fell fast asleep. He tiptoed into the stable where he found the three bridles. The bridles of silver and brass were very handsome, but Jean-Paul took the bridle made of steel, put it on the horse, and jumped on. The horse pawed the ground which made the lions wake up and roar. Jean-Paul tapped the horse with his hat and they soared through the air like the wind. Before the morning sun had risen in the sky, they were back at the king's castle.

Jean-Paul knocked on the door. "Madame, the queen," he called, "the horse with the grey beard is in the stable."

The wicked fairy was astonished and very angry. "How did you steal it from the twenty-five guardian lions? You are cunning indeed, my lad."

For a short time, the queen was gentle as a lamb. Then one morning, she woke in another fearful temper. She cursed and swore and smashed every cup in the castle.

"What is it now?" the king asked wearily.

"That boy is not learning a thing," she shrieked. "Unless he brings me the crystal chateau that hangs from three golden chains by daybreak, I want him hanged."

The king was unhappy, for he had grown fond of Jean-Paul, but there was nothing he could do.

Jean-Paul left the castle at once. He walked and walked until he came upon the old man watching his axe chop wood.

"Good day, sir," Jean-Paul called.

"Good day, my boy. You look weary. Come and rest."

"But I have a long search before me," said Jean-Paul. "I must find the crystal chateau that hangs from three golden chains and bring it to the wicked fairy before daybreak, or she will have me hanged."

"Never fear," said the old man, lowering his voice. "I can arrange it." He gave Jean-Paul supper, before he sent him on his way.

"Go straight along the road until you come to the green sea. There you will see the crystal chateau hanging by three golden chains above the water. It belongs to three evil fairies. It is their task to guard a wicker basket that holds the secret of the crystal chateau.

"Here is a little canoe made of paper; fold it and put it in your pocket. And here is a violin that will make even a donkey dance. Its song will serve you well. When you come to the green sea, eat these two small cakes and think of me. Then paddle the canoe to the chateau.

"Tell the three fairies that you have come in search of a wife and they will offer to pull you up to their balcony. Make them swear not to cut the rope once you are in the air. Wicked though they are, they always keep their promise.

"Do not marry the two older fairies; ask to marry the youngest and all will be well."

Jean-Paul thanked the old man and set off once more. He walked and walked until he came to the green sea. Then he took the paper canoe from his pocket, ate his two small cakes and thought of the old man. Instantly the canoe grew larger and he paddled it to the chateau.

Everything happened just as the old man had foretold. Once Jean-Paul had been pulled up to the balcony, the fairies asked which of the three he wished to marry.

He chose the youngest, who was also the smallest. Now marriages are made quickly in that country, so when they said, "Let us be married," they were.

"We must have a wedding feast," said Jean-Paul. "And I will play my violin."

"We don't know how to dance," said the fairies.

"That doesn't matter. My music makes everyone dance. My little wife will sit beside me." Jean-Paul began to play and the fairies danced.

"Stop, stop!" they gasped. But Jean-Paul played faster and faster until they fell to the ground unconscious. Then he picked them up and threw them into the sea.

"Why did you drown my sisters, husband?" the youngest fairy asked.

"I was afraid they would cause trouble between us. We will be happier by ourselves."

Jean-Paul remembered that he must look for the wicker basket. "Dear wife," he said, "show me the rest of the chateau."

One by one, she showed him six splendid rooms. When they came to the door of the seventh, she said, "This is not worth showing. It is just the same as the others."

But Jean-Paul insisted on seeing that room too. When the fairy opened the door, he saw a big black crow perched on a table. It was guarding the wicker basket.

"Tell me," he asked, "what is that?"

"That wicker basket will take the chateau wherever I wish," said the fairy. "If I turn it three times to the right and say, 'Basket so fair, pray take me there,' the chateau will go where I command."

"Tell me," said Jean-Paul, "what is in that small wooden box which sits inside the basket?"

"Two beautiful brown eyes," said his wife. "Once we were four fairies, sisters all. The oldest went in search of a husband and married Nicolas, the king's son. Those are the eyes of his first wife."

Jean-Paul could barely speak for rage, for he realized that they belonged to his mother.

"Tell me about the crow that watches over the basket," he said.

"That crow is the guardian of my sister's life. Break the crow's legs and her legs break too. Wring the crow's neck and her life is through."

"These stories are very strange," said Jean-Paul. "Tell me, can the eyes still see?"

"Yes, husband," said the fairy. "If someone who loved the owner put them back in their sockets, she would see again with the bright eyes of a young girl."

After they returned to the balcony, Jean-Paul picked up his violin and began to play. Unwillingly the fairy danced. Faster and faster he played until she cried, "Stop, stop! I can't dance anymore," and she fell to the ground unconscious. Jean-Paul threw her into the sea.

Then he ran back to the seventh room and seized the wicker basket. Turning it three times to the right, he said, "Basket so fair, pray take me there, to my father's house, the old hag's lair." At one stroke it was done.

Although the morning sun was still low in the sky, the king was walking alone in the garden. What should he see before him but the magnificent crystal chateau suspended in the air by three golden chains.

"Good day, sire," Jean-Paul called from the balcony. "I have brought the queen the crystal chateau. But first, would you like to see it?"

"Yes," said the king, and Jean-Paul lowered the rope and pulled him up.

"Sire," he said, "do you know who I am?"

"Certainly! You are the queen's young servant."

"No sire. I am your son. I came to find you and to take revenge on the wicked fairy for her evil deeds against my mother."

The king was overjoyed. "Is my Josette alive? Where is she?"

"I will take you to her, but first you must come with me."

Jean-Paul led his father to the seventh room of the chateau. Then he seized the crow and wrung its neck. At that very moment they heard the wicked fairy scream. They returned to the castle and found her dead on the floor.

While the king ordered his four black horses to be harnessed to the carriage, Jean-Paul climbed up to the crystal chateau to fetch the small wooden box.

They set off at once for the woodchopper's hut. When they arrived, the king wanted to go inside immediately.

"Wait, father," Jean-Paul said. "There is something I must do first."

He went inside. "Good day, Maman," he called.

"My dear son," cried Josette. "Is it really you?"

Jean-Paul went to his mother, opened her eyelids, and lovingly set her eyes in their sockets. Josette saw at once with the eyes of a young girl.

The king could wait no longer. He rushed into the hut and embraced his wife.

"Now," said the king, "I must reward the kind people who cared for you." He turned to the woodchopper and his wife, who stood shyly in the corner, and gave them a bag of gold.

Then they all set off for the city. On the way they stopped to get the old man who was still sitting on a stump watching his axe chop wood. When they reached the castle, the king ordered that a splendid feast be held in the crystal chateau. But Jean-Paul noticed that his mother looked sad.

"I have almost everything I could want," said Josette.

He knew what his mother still longed for. "Since your parents cannot come to us," he said, "we will go to them."

He ran to fetch the wicker basket, turned it three times to the right, and said, "Basket so fair, pray take me there, to my grandparents' house, there's no time to spare."

At one stroke it was done. The crystal chateau hung by its three golden chains above the small cottage.

Josette's father and mother came rushing to the door. They could not believe their eyes when they saw that their beautiful Josette, the king, and a fine young grandson had come to visit them at last.

Jean-Paul threw down the rope and pulled his grandparents up to the chateau. That evening they had a second feast more splendid than the first. Now Josette's happiness was complete, and everyone lived happily ever after.